TERRIFIC!

Sophie Gilmore

GREENWILLOW BOOKS
An Imprint of HarperCollins*Publishers*

Sennelier watercolors and Staedtler pens
were used to prepare the full-color artwork.
The text type is 20-point Wilke 55 Roman.

Library of Congress Cataloging-in-Publication Data

Names: Gilmore, Sophie, author, illustrator.
Title: Terrific / written and illustrated by Sophie Gilmore.
Description: First edition. | New York, NY : Greenwillow Books, an imprint of
HarperCollins Publishers, [2021] |
Audience: Ages 4–8. | Audience: Grades 2–3. |
Summary: "Mandrill, Owl, Badger, Turtle, and Anteater
try to find something terrific to do together,
as they discover that Snake has different ideas"
— Provided by publisher.
Identifiers: LCCN 2020025571 | ISBN 9780063025189 (hardcover)
Subjects: CYAC: Animals—Fiction. | Individuality—Fiction.
Predatory animals—Fiction.
Classification: LCC PZ7.1.G572 Ter 2021 | DDC [E]—dc23
LC record available at https://lccn.loc.gov/2020025571

First Edition

21 22 23 24 25 RTLO 10 9 8 7 6 5 4 3 2 1

GREENWILLOW BOOKS

For Leo,
a rather terrific animal.
And Philbs, who told me
Badger's eyes were wrong.

Five friends could not decide what to do.
"It should be something TERRIFIC!"
said Turtle.
They each thought hard about what
was terrific.

Anteater spoke first.
"Climbing is terrific.
You are as tall as the hills,
and can see them bustle with life."

So the friends tried climbing.

"Terrific," sighed Anteater.

But it was not terrific for them all.

"Swimming is terrific," announced Turtle.
"The water is cool and inviting, and you can push
your way through reeds, like an explorer."

So the friends
tried swimming.

"Terrific," sighed Turtle.
But it was not
terrific for them all.

Just then, Snake slithered close.
"*I* think that squeezing things tightly
in my coils is terrific."

"Thank you, Snake," said the friends,
"but we have no coils. Join us.
We'll find something terrific soon."

It was Owl's turn.
"Soaring in the sky is terrific.
You can tumble and roll,
and feel the wind in your wings."

"Wings?" mocked Snake.
"Only silly birds have those."
And they all laughed until
Owl snapped her beak at them.

"Hanging from your toes sure is terrific," said Mandrill.

"The world looks topsy-turvy,
and your hands are free to comb your fur."
So the friends gave it a try.

"Terrific," sighed Mandrill.

But it was not terrific for them all.

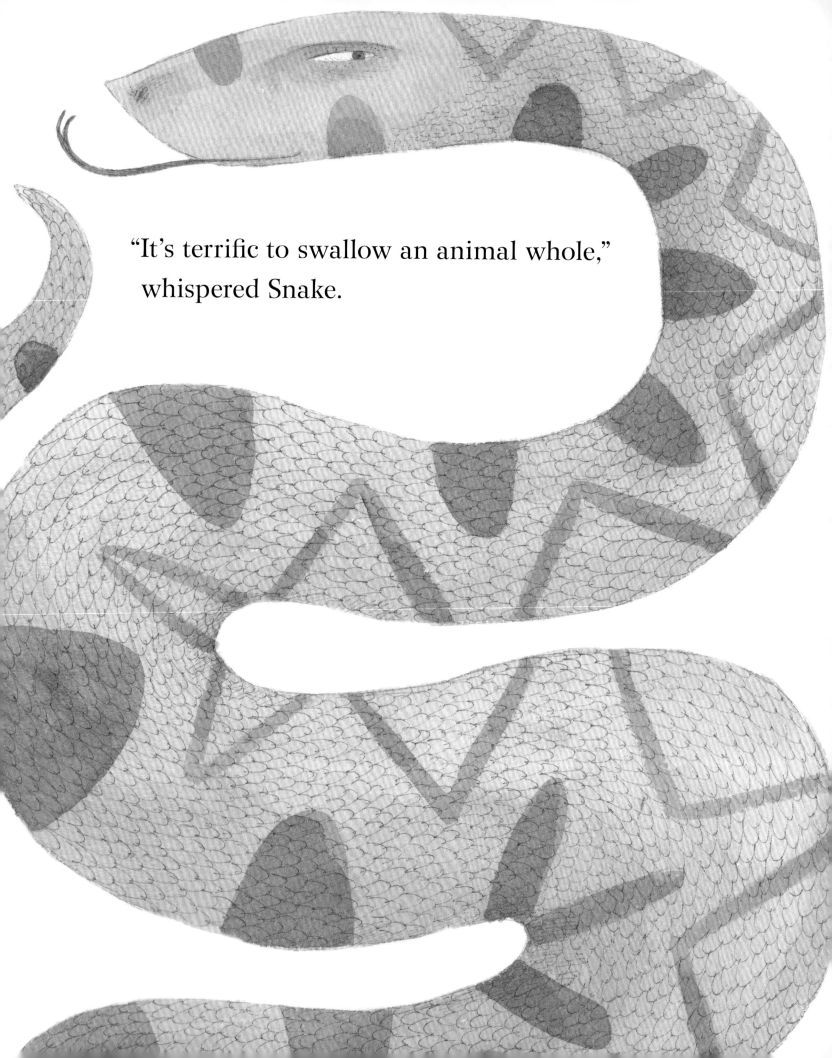

"It's terrific to swallow an animal whole,"
whispered Snake.

The friends were quiet.

"DIGGING IS ABSOLUTELY TERRIFIC!"
Badger yelled into the silence.

So the friends tried digging.

"Terrific," sighed Badger.

But it was not terrific
for them all.

Finding something terrific to do
had taken all day.
The friends were worn out.

A little glum, they collapsed together.

Except for Snake,
who hissed . . .

"EATING TOGETHER IS

TERRIFIC

and moved in to swallow them whole!

But with a beat of her wings,
Owl broke free.

She scooped Snake up in her beak,
and cried, "Eating together *IS* terrific!"

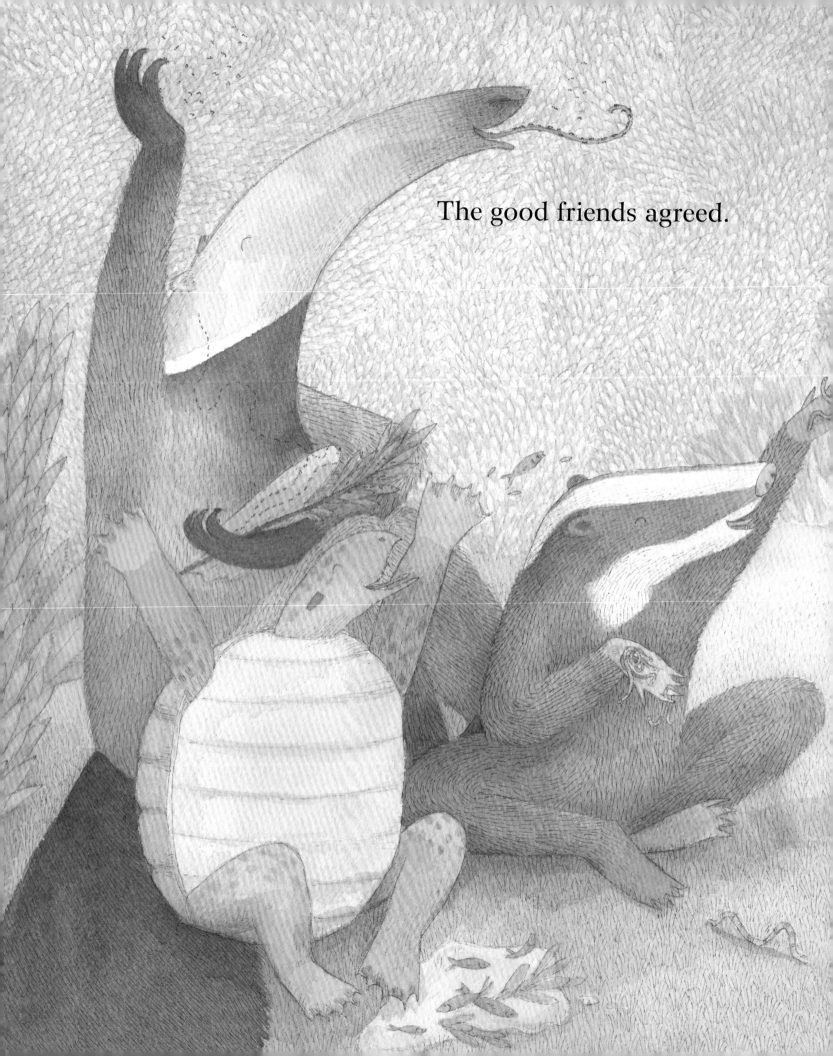

The good friends agreed.

"TERRIFIC!"